The babies turned and stared at Angelica. It was true! Water was pouring down where the babies were playing, but Angelica was nice and dry.

"How'd Angelica do that?" Chuckie asked as the babies scrambled out of the sandbox. They toddled over toward Angelica.

"Maybe Angelica's a witch," Phil suggested. "You know, like that one on TV that has—"

"Magic powers," Lil finished.

Rugrats Chapter Books

Angelica the GRAPE

**KLASKY
CSUPO** INC.

Based on the TV series *Rugrats*® created by Arlene Klasky, Gabor Csupo,
and Paul Germain as seen on Nickelodeon®

SIMON SPOTLIGHT

An imprint of Simon & Schuster Children's Publishing Division
1230 Avenue of the Americas, New York, New York 10020

Manufactured in the United States of America

First Edition

2 4 6 8 10 9 7 5 3 1

ISBN 0-689-83168-4

Library of Congress Catalog Card Number 99-76381

Angelica the GRAPE

by Nancy Krulik
illustrated by Joe Schiettino

Simon Spotlight/Nickelodeon

New York   London   Toronto   Sydney   Singapore

Chapter 1

Tommy Pickles wiped the sweat from his forehead and sighed. "It's really hot out here," he said to his friends as he dug his plastic yellow shovel deep into the sandbox.

"Yeah, it's hard work to dig the biggest hole in the world," added Phil.

Chuckie nodded. "Maybe we should stop digging, Tommy," Chuckie said. "Who knows what's down there. There could be monsters—big monsters with big red eyes, and sharp teeth, and . . ." Chuckie stopped talking and started shaking. He'd scared himself!

"Maybe there's ice-cream oceans and cookie trees down there," Tommy said, trying to calm Chuckie. "And we'll never know if we don't keep digging."

"Tommy's right," Phil told Chuckie. "We have to—"

"Keep digging," Phil's twin sister, Lil, completed her brother's thought. She grabbed the red shovel from Phil and began to dig.

"That's mine!" Phil shouted.

"You have to share, Philip," Lil told him. "Mommy always says so."

"Stop grabbing, Lillian," Phil answered. "That's what Mommy always says."

"Does not," Lil argued.

"Does too," Phil shouted back.

Tommy's cousin, Angelica, had been sitting under a tree watching the babies dig. She was getting bored. Angelica wanted to play a game. But she needed the babies to play with her.

Angelica walked over, put her arm around Chuckie, and smiled at him.

Chuckie looked up nervously at Angelica. Angelica was never nice to him—unless she wanted something. What did she want now?

"Chuckie's right, you know," Angelica told Tommy, Phil, and Lil. "There *are* monsters down there. And they are *really* scary. They're big and fat, and they're so tall, they can look right into your bedroom window—without standing on their tiptoes!"

"I gotta get outta here!" Chuckie cried. He scrambled out of the sandbox, took off his glasses, and wiped them anxiously.

Angelica smiled. Here was her chance to suggest that the babies play her game! "I know a nice, safe game that we can all play," Angelica told the babies. "It's called Castle."

"How do you play that?" Lil asked.

"Well . . . I pretend that I am a queen living in a big castle," Angelica said as she began to dance around the yard, pretending to hold up the skirt of an imaginary ball gown.

"What do we pretend to be?" Tommy asked his big cousin.

"That's the fun part." Angelica stopped dancing and stared at the babies. "You all get to pretend to be my servants. You have to do everything *I* tell you to do, because *I'm* the queen," she explained.

Tommy frowned. Castle sounded just like all the other games Angelica tried to get the babies to play. "That's no fun," he said. "I think I'll keep digging."

"Fine!" Angelica said. "Just don't come crying to me if a giant monster jumps up and scares your baby brother!" She pointed up toward Tommy's room, where his little brother, Dil, was sleeping soundly in his crib.

Tommy thought for a minute. His mom, Didi, was in the kitchen. His dad, Stu, was in his basement workshop, and his Grandpa Lou was busy sleeping in front of the TV. With all those grown-ups at home, Dil seemed pretty safe. So did Tommy and the other babies.

"No thanks, Angelica," Tommy told his cousin. "I don't think any monsters are going to get us. You're just trying to scare us."

Phil and Lil picked up their shovels and joined Tommy in the sandbox. Only

Chuckie stood outside the box. He looked from his friends to Angelica. Finally he decided that his place was beside his best friend. Chuckie climbed into the sandbox and once again began to shovel the sand.

Angelica put her hands on her hips. She was mad. "You babies are going to be sorry!" she warned.

Tommy, Phil, and Lil ignored Angelica. But Chuckie glanced over and gulped. This was not good. When Angelica got mad, she was much more dangerous than any monster could ever be!

Chapter 2

Angelica stormed angrily across the yard and sat down in the shade. As she combed the hair of her doll Cynthia, she tried to think of ways to make the babies sorry. "I could tie all their shoelaces together," she said. Then she shook her head. "That wouldn't work, 'cause I don't know how to tie shoelaces. Maybe I . . ."

Before Angelica could finish her

thought, she heard a loud clicking noise. Suddenly a burst of water came up from the grass. The water was only shooting up in the area near the sandbox. Angelica knew that the water was coming from the new automatic underground sprinkler system Stu had put in. It was just like the one at her house. The sprinkler turned on all by itself. Water popped up in different areas of the yard throughout the day.

But the babies did not know that the water was coming from an underground sprinkler system. All they knew was that their huge hole in the sand was filling up with water.

"It's raining!" Chuckie shouted to the others. He hadn't noticed that the water was coming up from the ground instead of from the sky. "Let's go inside before we get all wet."

"Hey! We don't have to go inside," Lil said.

"Yeah, look. It's not raining where Angelica is," Phil added.

The babies turned and stared at Angelica. It was true! Water was pouring down where the babies were playing, but Angelica was nice and dry.

"How'd Angelica do that?" Chuckie asked as the babies scrambled out of the sandbox. They toddled over toward Angelica.

Tommy shook his head. "I dunno," he said. "But there's lotsa reasons why it's raining here and not there."

"Like what?" Chuckie asked.

Tommy scratched his head. "Well . . . I'm sure there must be one."

"Maybe Angelica's a witch," Phil suggested. "You know, like that one on TV that has—"

"Magic powers," Lil finished.

Chuckie started to shake again. It was bad enough that Angelica was bigger than they were. If she had magic powers too, then she could . . . Chuckie tried to stop his brain from thinking. It was too scary! "Tommy . . ." he began nervously.

"Shh," Tommy warned. "Don't let Angelica know you're a-scared of her."

But it was too late. Angelica had already overheard the babies. She smirked. "See? I told you babies that you were going to be sorry," she said. "I made it rain on you—with my magic powers! Now your big old hole is all full of water."

Angelica began to laugh, "Ha, ha, ha, ha, ha."

Tommy stared at his cousin. "How come you never showed us your magic powers before, Angelica?" he asked.

Angelica thought quickly. "Because I

just got 'em!" she said. "I had to wait till today before I could use my powers."

"Wow! Are we gonna get powers too?" Lil asked.

Angelica shook her head. "No," she said, "you have to be 'specially picked to get magic powers. Now, if you want me to make the rain stop, you have to do as I say. Otherwise that whole sandbox is going to be a pile of mush!"

Chuckie stood by Angelica's side. "I'm sorry, Angelica," he apologized quickly. "I'll play Castle with you."

Angelica smiled. "Smart move, Finster," she said. Then she turned to Tommy and the twins. "And how about you babies?"

Tommy looked at the big wet puddle behind him. He had no choice—he had to play Angelica's game. Tommy nodded his head. So did Phil and Lil.

Tommy looked over at the grass around the sandbox. The water was still hitting it pretty hard. "Okay, we said we'd play with you," Tommy told Angelica. "How come you're not stopping the rain?"

Angelica gulped. She didn't have an answer for that one. She didn't know how to turn the sprinkler off! Angelica kicked at the grass by her feet, and her foot tapped something hard. It was the hidden sprinkler switch! Suddenly the automatic sprinkler turned off.

The babies gasped.

"Wow!" Chuckie exclaimed.

"Did you see that?" Lil asked Phil.

Now even Tommy had to believe that his cousin had magic powers. "That was really amazing, Angelica," he said.

Angelica smiled, then shook her head. "You can't call me Angelica anymore," she said. "I am the leader of this bunch.

From now on, you babies have to call me Angelica the Great! If you don't, I'll use my magic powers to squish you!"

Chuckie was still too amazed by the fact that Angelica had stopped the rain to hear what she had just proclaimed. "What did she say?" he whispered to Tommy.

"She wants us to call her Angelica the Grape," Tommy said.

"Why?" Chuckie whispered back.

"She says we're part of her bunch," Tommy replied. "I guess that makes her the head grape. She does look like a grape in that purple dress."

Calling Angelica a grape seemed pretty silly to Chuckie, but he wasn't about to argue with her. Now that she had magic powers, none of the babies were willing to question the all-powerful Angelica the Grape!

Chapter 3

"Chuckie! Get me a drink. Now!"

Chuckie started to shake whenever he heard Angelica's voice coming from the lounge chair she'd placed beneath the tree in the backyard.

Angelica had been ordering the babies around all morning.

"Yes, Angelica," he answered as he headed toward the kitchen.

"Now, Finster, what did you call me?"

Angelica demanded.

"Um, I mean, yes, Angelica the Grape," Chuckie said.

"Not Angelica the Grape. Angelica the *Great*," she corrected. "Now, move it!"

Chuckie raced into the kitchen as quickly as he could.

"Hmm, let's see," Angelica said as she looked around for her next victim. Her eyes rested on Phil and Lil. "You two," she said, calling the twins to her side. "Cynthia and I would like a little entertainment. I order you both to sing Cynthia's favorite song."

"What song is that?" Phil asked her.

Angelica sighed. "Cynthia's favorite song is the song from the Cynthia commercials."

"I don't know it," Phil said.

"Me either," Lil admitted.

Angelica sighed again and sat up.

"I *have* to teach you babies everything, don't I?" she asked impatiently.

Then she began to sing, "I am Cynthia, buy me, buy me! Here are the things I can be: a doctor, a teacher, a vet who won't hurt a flea. I don't need a diploma or a college degree. Just lots of outfits, that you can buy me . . . buy me!"

When Angelica finished the song, Phil and Lil clapped. "That was nice, Angelica," Phil said.

Angelica glared at Phil.

"I mean that was nice, Angelica the Grape," Phil corrected himself.

"It's Angelica the *Great*! *Great*, not grape! Oh, never mind." Angelica sighed. She settled back into the chair and placed Cynthia on her lap. "Now you two sing the song."

Phil and Lil stood by Angelica's chair. They took a deep breath and began to sing, "I am Cynthia, buy me, buy me . . ."

Just then Chuckie came back outside carrying two purple juice boxes.

"Oh, goody, grape juice!" Angelica shouted. "Hurry and bring it over here!"

"Yes, Angelica the Grape," Chuckie replied. He ran across the lawn. Tommy's dog, Spike, who had been sleeping nearby, woke up. He thought Chuckie was playing with him. Spike ran after Chuckie and jumped up.

"Spike! No!" Tommy yelled.

But it was too late. Spike banged into Chuckie. Chuckie tripped and fell. One of the two juice boxes flew out of Chuckie's arms and landed—*splat!*—right on Angelica. The sticky purple juice spilled all over Angelica's dress.

"Now you really are Angelica the Grape!" Tommy cried, trying not to laugh.

Angelica made a face. "Well, at least there is still one juice box that hasn't been squished," she said as she grabbed the other juice box from Chuckie's hands and began drinking from the straw.

"Uh, Angelica, that's mine," Chuckie said. "I started drinking it."

Angelica began to cough. She coughed so hard, grape juice came out of her nose. "Blech! Baby germs!" she said. Then she picked up the straw from the empty juice box that lay on her lounge chair. She placed it in Chuckie's juice box, sat back, and took a sip. "Ahhh . . . that's better," she said. Then she turned to Tommy. "Come here."

Tommy toddled over to his cousin. Angelica handed him the juice box. "Hold this for me," she said.

Tommy held the box while Angelica

sucked the juice from the straw. Tommy frowned. He wasn't sure how much more of Angelica the Grape he would be able to take.

Just then Didi came outside. She had five frozen fruit juice pops in her hands. "I thought you sweeties might like a cold treat," she told Angelica and the babies as she handed each of them a pop. Then she went back inside.

"Yummy!" Tommy exclaimed as he got ready to take a lick of his pop.

"Oh, no you don't!" Angelica cried out, grabbing the pop from Tommy. "That's mine. All those pops are mine!"

"Why?" Tommy demanded.

"Because I am Angelica the Great. Everything belongs to me," Angelica said.

Tommy reached over and took the pop back from Angelica. "I don't want to play Castle anymore!"

Chuckie stared at his friend. "Tommy, what are you doing?" Chuckie asked. "She might use her powers on you!"

"I don't care," Tommy said. "Sometimes a baby's gotta do what a baby's gotta do. I'm hot. So I gotta eat my fruit juice pop."

"Me too!" Lil declared.

"Me too!" Phil added.

Angelica popped up from her chair. "You babies are going to be *sooo* sorry," she shouted. She began waving her arms wildly, pretending to create some very dangerous magic.

To everyone's surprise—including Angelica's—the sprinkler went on again in a different corner of the yard.

Angelica's eyes opened wide. She was amazed at her good luck. Now the babies would really be afraid of her!

"See what I did!" She smirked.

Tommy grinned. "Thanks, Angelica!"

Angelica watched as her little cousin ran over to the water and began to play in the sprinkler. Chuckie, Phil, and Lil followed him.

"Look at me!" Phil shouted to the others. He filled his mouth with water and then spit it out in a long stream. He looked like a baby water fountain.

"I want to try that!" Lil said as she tried to copy her brother.

"Oooh . . . I got cold water in my diapie!" Tommy giggled.

As Angelica watched the babies play in the water, she got angrier. Things were not going the way she'd planned— but she wasn't about to give up!

"You babies better be careful!" she told them. "I'm just getting started!"

Chapter 4

Angelica wandered into Tommy's house. As she walked down the hall, she tried to come up with a new plan to make the babies do what she wanted them to do. But she couldn't think of a thing. Finally she plopped herself down on a big couch to rest. Thinking was tiring!

Suddenly Angelica spotted a small, black, rectangular object sitting on the coffee table. She'd seen something just like that in her mother's pocketbook. It was a car remote control. Her mother used it to open the car doors and turn on the car lights. She didn't even have to be near the car to do it. Angelica smiled. The car remote control worked like . . . magic!

Angelica giggled happily as she scooped the remote control from the table and placed it in the front pocket of her dress. Then she raced back out into the yard.

As Angelica came outside, she saw the babies playing in the sprinkler. Their tongues were all red from the fruit juice pops, and their hair and clothes were wet. They looked like they were having a lot of fun—without her!

"Okay, babies, I warned you!" she called out. "Now I am really going to put my magic powers to work!"

Angelica ran back into the house, toward the front door. She held the car remote control where no one could see it. Then she pushed one of the buttons. There was a loud beep. Angelica waited for the babies to come running over to see where the noise was coming from. But they didn't. So she pushed the button again . . . and again. Finally Angelica heard their footsteps. She pushed another button. The car's headlights flashed on. Angelica pushed the button again. The lights went off.

Chuckie was the first one to spot the car outside the window.

"T-T-T-Tommy, did you see that?" Chuckie stammered.

Tommy looked, but he didn't see anything. "See what?" he asked.

Angelica pushed a button. The car lights flashed on and off. She pushed

another button. The windshield wipers began swishing back and forth.

"That car is alive!" Phil cried out.

"AHHHHH!" The babies all screamed.

Angelica smiled. "I told you babies to play my game," she said. "Now I've brought this car to life. It's my servant. And it will do whatever I tell it to!"

Chuckie looked at the car. Its lights were still flashing, and the windshield wipers were moving faster than ever. "Angelica, please tell the car to stop. I'll play Castle with you, I promise!" Chuckie pleaded.

"Me too!" Phil and Lil said at once.

Tommy looked from Angelica to the car. He had no choice. "Okay, Angelica," he said finally. "Let's play Castle."

Chapter 5

Angelica and the babies played Castle for the rest of the day. Finally Didi and Stu came out to the yard. Didi was carrying Dil in her arms.

"Okay, you guys," Stu said. "It's time to go inside now."

Tommy was glad. The babies would be safe inside the house. And Tommy was sure that Angelica would not use her magic in front of his mommy and daddy.

Angelica never did anything mean when grown-ups were around.

Tommy was right. As soon as they entered the house, Angelica didn't say anything about magic powers.

Instead she sat down in front of the TV and watched the *Ho Ho the Clown Show*. Angelica never missed it.

It wasn't that she liked the clown. Angelica watched Ho Ho because at least three Cynthia doll commercials always came on during the show. Angelica needed to watch the commercials. How else would she know what to ask her mommy and daddy to buy for her?

While Angelica watched TV, the babies played happily on the floor. Phil rolled a ball toward Lil. Lil rolled the ball back to Phil, but the ball moved right past him and into the hall. Phil ran to grab the ball.

Just then they all heard Phil cry out, "Oh, no!"

Lil, Tommy, and Chuckie looked over at Phil.

"What happened?" Tommy asked.

"The sun is going away," Phil called back. "We're going to have to go home soon."

"And we were just starting to have fun!" Tommy said.

"Shh," Chuckie whispered. "Angelica the Grape will hear you. And you never know what she'll do with her powers!"

"Angelica the Grape," Tommy muttered. "That's it, Chuckie!"

Chuckie looked curiously at Tommy. "What's it?" he asked.

"*Angelica* can bring the sun back," replied Tommy.

"How are you going to get her to do that?" wondered Chuckie.

"I'll ask her to," Tommy said simply.

Tommy walked across the room. "Angelica the Grape, can you help us?" he asked.

"What do you want?" Angelica replied.

"Well, I was wondering, how strong are your magic powers?"

"Really strong," Angelica told him.

"Are they stronger than the sun?" Tommy continued.

"Sure they are!" Angelica assured him.

"Really?" Tommy said. "Can you make the sun come back? It's almost gone, and we want to play some more."

Angelica was trapped. She didn't know how to make the sun come back. But Angelica knew that if she didn't do something, the babies would stop believing that she had magic powers.

She started pacing back and forth.

"I don't know if I should help you," she said. But what Angelica was really thinking was what she was going to do next.

"Oh, please, Angelica the Grape," pleaded Tommy.

Just then Angelica had a bright idea. "Oh, all right," she said. "But you babies have to stay here. I'm going outside to order the sun to shine!"

And with that, Angelica headed out to the front porch.

Tommy and the other babies gathered in the living room and waited for Angelica to return.

"Do you think she can really do it, Tommy?" Phil asked.

"She says she can," Tommy replied.

Finally, Angelica came skipping back into the living room. "You babies can all thank me now," she said. "The sun is back! Go look out the window by the front door. You'll see."

Angelica followed the babies toward the window. Sure enough, it was bright as morning on the porch.

"Wow!" Phil said.

"Yeah, wow!" Lil said.

"Angelica, you really are the grapest!" Chuckie declared.

"How'd you do it?" Tommy asked.

Angelica crossed her fingers behind her back and smiled. "Magic!" she declared as she glanced over at the light switch on the far end of the porch. All Angelica had really done was turn on the porch light. And now it looked just like the sun was shining on the porch.

These babies are so easy to fool, Angelica thought.

Chapter 6

The next morning it was raining. Didi had gone grocery shopping with Phil and Lil's mother, Betty. Stu was in his workshop. Grandpa Lou was supposed to be watching the babies, but he had fallen asleep on the couch.

For a while, Tommy and his friends played catch with baby Dil. Dil threw his blue teddy bear out of his playpen, and the babies threw it back. Of course Dil never caught the bear.

One of the babies would have to pick it up and hand it to Dil. Then Dil would throw the bear again, and the babies would throw it back again. It was fun at first, but the babies soon tired of the game. What they really wanted to do was play outside.

"I wish Angelica were here," Chuckie said. "She could make the rain stop."

The other babies stared at Chuckie. They couldn't believe he was wishing for Angelica.

Suddenly the doorbell rang. Stu ran up from his workshop and opened the door. "Hello, Drew," he said. "Hi, Angelica."

The babies rushed over excitedly. Drew smiled and patted his daughter's head. "The babies sure are glad to see you, princess," he said.

"Of course they are, Daddy. Who wouldn't be?" Angelica replied.

Just then the phone rang. But Tommy's dad didn't rush to answer it. "I'll let the machine get it," Stu told Drew.

After a while, Drew left and Stu took baby Dil with him back down to the basement.

Angelica walked into the living room and sat down on the floor. The babies stood around her.

"We need you to stop the rain," Phil said.

"Right now," Lil added.

Angelica gulped. This was a problem. She didn't know how to stop real rain.

Before Angelica could reply, Stu called out from the kitchen, "Hey, kids, I'm going to bring you a snack."

Angelica breathed a sigh of relief. She

was saved—for a while, anyway.

Stu handed each child a chocolate chip cookie. Angelica began to pout. Here she was, a big girl, and she was getting the same number of cookies as the babies. Angelica thought she deserved a lot more cookies.

She frowned for a second, and then she smiled. She had a great idea! "Hey, babies," she said. "How would *you* like to have magic powers?"

Chapter 7

The babies stared at Angelica. Was she really going to give them powers?

"You mean you'll show us how to stop the rain?" Lil asked.

Angelica shook her head. "No. That's only for big kids to know. But I can show you other things."

"What do we have to do?" Tommy asked.

"You have to give me one cookie for

each magic power," Angelica said.

The babies quickly turned over their cookies to Angelica. She stuffed them into her mouth one by one. Then she said to the babies, "Okay, follow me!"

Angelica led them into the living room. She pointed to a big white box. "Do you miss your mommy, Tommy?" she asked.

Tommy nodded.

"Well, she can talk to you right now, even though she's not here. Just make a wish to hear your mommy's voice. Then push that green button."

Tommy closed his eyes and wished to hear Didi's voice. Then he pushed the button. Suddenly his mother's voice came out of the machine. "Stu, where are you? I called to check on the kids. Are you there?"

"Wow!" Tommy said, amazed. "I did it!

My mommy's talking to me!"

Tommy pushed the button a second time. Once again, he heard his mother's voice. "Stu, where are you . . ."

Angelica then took Chuckie, Phil, and Lil and walked into the bathroom. "You're going to be really powerful," Angelica told Lil.

"I am?" said Lil, looking puzzled.

"Yeah, you're going to make a storm!" said Angelica as she pointed to the toilet. "Now, you're in charge of this storm. Just push that silver thing down."

Lil toddled over to the toilet and flushed. Whoosh! The toilet made a loud gurgling noise. Then the water began swirling around and around like a tornado.

"Wow!" Lil exclaimed. "I am powerful!"

As Lil created storm after storm in the toilet bowl, Angelica, Chuckie, and

Phil went into Grandpa Lou's bedroom. "Do you want to make that box sing?" she asked Chuckie as she pointed to Grandpa Lou's clock radio.

Chuckie nodded.

"Okay, say abracadabra. Then hit that button," Angelica told him. She pointed to the on switch.

"Abracadabra!" Chuckie cried out as he hit the button. Music blared through the room. Chuckie was so shocked that he knocked over the radio. The music stopped.

"Was that part of my powers?" Chuckie asked Angelica.

Angelica was worried. If the radio was broken, she didn't want to be blamed for it. "I'm not sure," she replied, pushing Phil out the door. "Come on, Phil. I'll give you a magic power!"

Chuckie stared at the radio. No sound

was coming from it at all. Then suddenly another song blasted out. It was really, really loud. "Shh," he told the radio. "Stop singing."

But the music kept playing. "Abra-cadabra, abracadabra," Chuckie repeated quickly as he pushed at all the buttons. The radio finally stopped.

"Whew," said Chuckie. He turned to leave the room, but before he got through the door, the radio began to play again!

"Arrghhh . . ." cried Chuckie. He went back to try to stop the radio from playing.

While Chuckie was struggling with the clock radio, Angelica and Phil were in the living room. She popped a videotape into the VCR.

"You can make all the people on TV do what you want," she told Phil as she

handed him the remote control for the VCR. "Just use this. It will give you magic powers."

Phil pushed one button. The people on the TV screen moved really, really fast. Then he pushed a different button. The people on the screen were still moving fast, but they were going backward!

Now that the babies were busy with their magic powers, Angelica snuck into the kitchen. It was time to get more cookies! But before she could stick her hand into the cookie jar, the front door opened.

Didi and Betty were home.

Chapter 8

"What's going on, Pop?" Didi asked Grandpa Lou as she walked into the house. She could hear her own voice echoing over and over again from the answering machine.

Grandpa Lou woke up. "What in tarnation?" he exclaimed as he heard music blaring from his clock radio.

In the living room, Betty found Phil speeding the videotape forward and backward. And when she walked past the bathroom, she discovered Lil excitedly flushing the toilet again and again.

"Looks like the little ponies got out of the corral," Betty remarked to Didi. "Good thing this rain stopped."

Angelica overheard Betty—and that gave her one more idea. "Hey, you babies," Angelica cried out. "Come here."

The babies came running to Angelica's side. She smiled at them. "Since you all did so well with your magic powers, I'm going to give you a special treat," Angelica said. "I am going to stop the rain!"

Angelica waved her arms in the air. Then Didi walked into the room.

"It's stopped raining," Didi said. "You can all go outside and play now."

The babies grinned and hurried

toward the backyard. Angelica gave a huge sigh. It wasn't easy being so powerful.

"Isn't Mother Nature amazing, Deed?" Betty said. "One minute it's raining cats and dogs, the next minute the sun is shining."

"I wonder who Mother Nature's kid is," Angelica said to her doll Cynthia. "He's lucky to have a mommy who can *really* stop the rain! That would be *sooo* great!"

About the Author

Nancy Krulik is the author of more than one hundred books for children and young adults, including a few based on the hit Nickelodeon TV series, *Rugrats* and *CatDog*. She has also written for several Nick Jr. TV shows, including *Gullah Gullah Island* and *Eureeka's Castle*.

Nancy lives in Manhattan with her husband, Danny, her two kids, Amanda and Ian, and a guinea pig named Tutankhamen. Between writing books and taking care of her family, Nancy often wishes that she had *real* magic powers to help her out. But for now, she'll settle for the magic of the dishwasher, the washing machine, the TV remote, and the computer!